Bootsie

and the Tourists

MIKE JAMES

Text copyright © Mike James 2011
ISBN: 9781921787676
Published by Vivid Publishing
P.O. Box 948, Fremantle
Western Australia 6959
www.vividpublishing.com.au

Chapters

1

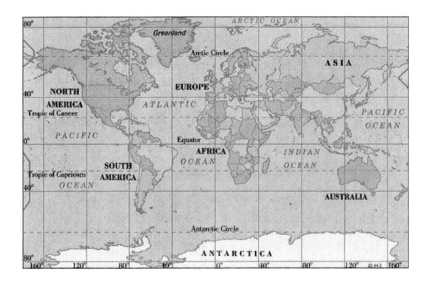

Bootsie Hits
The Spot

"Well, at least we all hit the board anyway," said the coach as the three of them walked towards the map on the back of the door.

"Yours is a bit wet coach, no rugby in the Indian Ocean," the headmaster said jokingly, as he looked closer.

"Well I don't think they play in Greenland either, looking at where your dart has landed," replied the coach.

"Ooh too cold anyway. The arthritis in my knees would give me terrible trouble if we went there," added the headmaster. "Bootsie's hit the spot by the look of it. Yes, good shot, son," said a joyful headmaster.

"Is that it? Does that mean we're going on tour there next year?" asked a very excited Bootsie.

"Yes son, that's exactly where we'll be going. I'll start organising it as soon as possible," replied the headmaster.

"First things first however," said the coach.

"What do you mean?" asked Bootsie.

"Well, before we can think about the overseas trip next year, we'd better finish the rest of the games in this season first and don't forget we've got the visiting overseas school side coming to All Kings this year as well," added the coach.

Bootsie wasn't sure if it was a good idea to tell the rest of the school that he knew where they were going for next year's trip, so he decided to keep the little secret to himself. A few days later at an assembly, the headmaster announced that he had made a decision about the trip and the school's rugby team would be heading on tour for two games against Charlton Hall, the same team that would be visiting the school this season. Actually, he said to the boys that he had sat and thought about the destination long and hard before making his decision. Bootsie grinned to himself when he heard this. "If only they really knew," he thought to himself.

There was a huge buzz going around the school after the announcement was made. What Bootsie didn't know was that quite a few non-players were also chosen to go on the trip to help out the team and there would be many competitions in the future to see who actually got to go. To keep his place in the team, Bootsie would need to continue his good efforts on and off the field in order to get to travel. Not everything was a certainty at All Kings. At least next year Bootsie would only be competing against boys in his own age group and boys who were a year younger, so he felt a bit better about keeping his place in the team.

As the coach had said in the headmaster's office, they still had to think about the rest of the games in this season first, including the dreaded away game at St David's. He had been told that away games at St David's could make him feel like he was a soldier who had been dropped behind enemy lines. Bootsie couldn't wait for the return game to see if it was going to be as bad as everyone was telling him it would be.

The private schoolboy competition was very different to other competitions Bootsie was used to playing in. There were no quarter, semi or grand final games to play in; there were simply fourteen rounds in the season with each team in turn, getting a bye. Some teams you played twice and some only once. The team at the top of the ladder was the winner of the competition for that season. If two teams finished on the same points, there would be a play off to decide the winning team for that year.   His coach explained to him how important bonus points were each game and they could be the difference between winning and losing the prized trophy.

This week All Kings were playing away against Westchester College, Bootsie now realized how important it was to win each and every game to get to and stay on top of the ladder.   All Kings looked very impressive so far, with three wins from their first three games of the season.

There were ten private schools in the region and each one of the schools had a team in the competition.   All Kings, St Benedict's and Westchester all had a good start and were the top three teams in the senior and junior competition. It was still very early in the season and no team could rest easy on their current performances. Any number of teams could end up at the top of the ladder by the end of the season and claim the premiership. Currently the junior boys' ladder in this week's Gazette looked like this.

Junior Boys Ladder – Week 3

	P	W	L	D	B	F	A	Pts
Westchester College	3	3	0	0	3	120	37	15
Saint Benedicts	3	3	0	0	2	84	35	14
All Kings	3	3	0	0	1	52	10	13
St Mark's	3	2	1	0	1	62	67	9
St Josephs	3	1	2	0	1	41	50	5
St Luke's	3	1	2	0	1	59	94	5
Christian Boys	3	1	2	0	0	30	58	4
St David's	3	0	3	0	3	39	55	3
St Peter's	3	0	3	0	1	58	74	1
Bluedale College	3	0	3	0	1	39	104	1

Each week, the competition ladder was printed in the All Kings Gazette and if Bootsie wasn't being mentioned on either the front or back page, it was the next thing he would look at. He still hadn't played all the teams yet and wasn't sure which teams were the ones to look out for. He had been told not to worry about their next opponents, Westchester College, as they were all soft.

"If they're so soft, why are they first on the ladder with no losses so far?" he thought to himself, as he studied the ladder in The Gazette.

"They've scored a lot more points than we have, but they've also let more points be scored by the opposition, *a lot more*," Bootsie said to Razzi who was sitting on the end of Bootsie's bed reading his own copy of The Gazette.

"They're soft. Don't even worry about them," replied Razzi without looking up from his paper. "Look at our against points. *Ten.* In three games so far they've only managed to get *ten* points against us. It means our defence is superb and that's our strong point," added Razzi.

"I don't know. They've scored sixty-eight more points than we have in their three games so far," said Bootsie. "Depends who they've played. You'd have to get The Gazette from the last three weeks and see which of the other teams they've played. I bet they're all the teams down the bottom of the ladder," replied Razzi. "I'm going to," said Bootsie, as he left in search of the last three editions of the paper.

"You're wasting your time. I'm telling you Westchester College boys are soft," shouted Razzi, as Bootsie left the dormitory.

Bootsie went to the offices where the paper was printed and was given a copy of the recent fixtures from one of the boy reporters. He couldn't believe Razzi was right; so far, Westchester had played against St David's, bottom of the ladder Bluedale and St Luke's. Two teams at the bottom and one not far behind. Maybe he *was* worrying about nothing.

2

They're Soft

During the rugby season every second Saturday morning meant another bus trip to a different school for the next away game. Bootsie was really getting used to his new life on the rugby team at All Kings. He hadn't received any bad press since the first week against Christian Boys College and last week he was carried off as a hero after the game.

On each bus trip he would listen to music through his headphones, just like he had seen the Test players do when they were on their bus and arriving at the stadium before a big match. The music really helped with the nerves before a game and it pumped him up before he took to the field. They arrived at Westchester College and Bootsie couldn't help but notice how impressive the grounds of the school were. "All Kings is nice but this is something else altogether," he thought to himself as he looked out the window of the bus.

Westchester College was built in 1910 and has always been the premier College in the region. It is by far the most expensive of all the private schools you can go to, with a reputation that is reflected in the types of vehicles the students arrive in each year. The school colours are black and amber with the Latin motto of *'Caritas Christi'*, which means, 'The love of Christ' in English.

"Nice school," said Bootsie to Razzi as they got off the bus.

"Look Bootsie, they're rich, spoilt and soft. You'll see," replied Razzi. "Smash 'em hard and they'll crumble," he added, as he put his headphones back on his head.

Bootsie was also impressed with the school's changing rooms. All Kings had a good set up as well, but it was mainly for the home team. These were excellent conditions for both teams. By the noise coming from outside the change rooms, the All Kings players could hear the traveling circus had arrived and was in full voice. By the time Bootsie and the other junior boys ran onto the field, the supporters of the Westchester College were screaming wildly for their own team who had just taken to the field. Bootsie looked at the other team and didn't see anything soft-looking about any of the boys; most of them seemed very big for their age.

Once again, Bootsie was learning new things about himself, courtesy of a very fired up Westchester crowd and their colourful chants and songs about the opposition team. From the opening kick All Kings were under the pump. Their left-winger 'Socks', who never played with his socks pulled up, as was tradition at All Kings, caught the ball from the kick off and was immediately met by a wall of defenders. Before his teammates could get back to support him he had the ball stolen away from him and Westchester were surging towards the line. Bootsie got back in cover defence and held his ground on the All Kings goal line. The Westchester forwards kept up the strategy of picking and driving at the line. Luckily the All Kings boys were up to the challenge in defence.

The ball must have gone through at least twelve phases of play before they changed tack and spread the ball out wide to the backs. Bootsie raced off the goal line and tackled a Westchester player close to the All Kings 22 metre line. The home team had lost a good bit of ground but was still in good attacking territory. First blood to All Kings, they had stopped the opposition from scoring. Their excellent defence had resisted multiple phases of attack and forced the Westchester boys way back from the goal line.

They may have won that initial battle, but the war that day would be a long one. In the first half All Kings spent exactly ten minutes and twenty-five seconds inside the Westchester half and the remaining twenty-nine minutes and thirty-five seconds defending inside their own half. It was incredible defence by the All Kings boys and amazingly the score at half time was All Kings 0, Westchester 0.

"Boys, I can't believe you survived that onslaught for pretty much the entire first half and they still couldn't score. It's a credit to your defence," said the coach, as he addressed the boys at half time. "Those Westchester boys must be thinking they can't score against us. This game is ours for the taking, but we just need more possession this half. It's our kick off, so keep them down in their 22, strike early and strike hard, don't let up until we get the points on the board. If we can score early, they'll crack for sure," he added. Bootsie looked around the room; he could see most of the boys already looked exhausted. It had been a very tough first half, constantly defending the line and after last week's big effort against St David's he was very worried about the second half. It wouldn't take him long to realize his worries were very reasonable.

The kick off didn't go at all to plan and two minutes after the start of the second half All Kings was back defending hard on *their* goal line. Bootsie was giving it his all; he stayed very close to the rucks to push back a sea of black and amber attackers. When he went down in a tackle he would release the tackled player, roll away and would quickly get to his feet so he could get back to defend the line again. Each time the other All Kings defenders got up it was slower and slower and eventually the onslaught was too much and Westchester crossed the line for their first try of the day. It had taken them the entire first half and then some, but it did eventually come. After the conversion the score was All Kings 0, Westchester 7.

If it had taken the first half and then some for the All Kings defensive line to leak, then it only took a further thirty seconds for it to completely burst. Within another ten minutes

Westchester had crossed the line four more times, and the score quickly blew out to All Kings 0, Westchester 31. All Kings had used all their efforts defending the line and with all their players becoming involved, the Westchester backline had been cooling their heels waiting patiently for the ball to come out to them. For the rest of the game the ball was spread out wide to the outside backs and their fresh legs were too much for the tired chasers from All Kings. Even Bootsie who prided himself on his leg-strength and fitness had to look on as the Westchester backs ran rampant over All Kings.

It seemed like for the entire second half the All Kings boys were walking back to their in-goal area for the Westchester fly half to have a shot at goal. Heads down, hands on hips they were a beaten team.

"This is ridiculous," said John, the All Kings captain.

"Soft you reckon?" Bootsie said to an exhausted Razzi.

"Blah!" was all he could reply, as he sucked down more water from his water bottle.

Bootsie couldn't believe how the game had played out; they had been taught a lesson today, a rugby lesson. The final whistle couldn't come quick enough for All Kings and they walked off the field exhausted and beaten. The final Score that day was All Kings 0, Westchester 60. As they came together to clap off the Westchester team, the Westchester supporters came together as one and began to sing.

"WESTCHESTER, WESTCHESTER is where you came today, WESTCHESTER, WESTCHESTER is where you came to play, WESTCHESTER, WESTCHESTER next time you'll stay away!!!

"Yeah, yeah, winners are grinners," Bootsie thought to himself as he shook hands with the winning team's players. "I can't wait to read the headline that's going to be stuck to my wardrobe door in the morning," he thought.

The All Kin

Sunday Edition

JUNIOR BOYS FORGET T

All Kings junior side must have forgotten that rugby is played over two halves when they forgot to come out and play for the second half in yesterday's whitewash at Westchester. The superior Westchester forward pack left a bruised and battered All Kings team in its shadows as they ran rampant over a tired and helpless All Kings side. Things looked promising at the half time break with neither team being able to put points on the board. What was set up for a cracking second half quickly turned into a display of soft and weak defending by the All Kings team allowing Westchester to embarrass the junior side into a 60 to 0 final score.

Thankfully the senior boys redeemed the schools name by crushing the Westchester senior side 12 to 5, more on the senior boys crushing win in the sport section. Hopefully next week not only Socks will be pulling up his socks and putting in a better effort. Remember John, Bootsie and the rest of you junior boys there are two halves in a game and you should p

Ren
foll
imp

The
that
rele
the
beh
of s
exp
in t
its
beh
con
or v

It m
tota
thin
dec

The Press Is
At It Again

Bootsie lay in his bed with his back turned to his wardrobe. "Surely they couldn't criticize yesterday's effort could they? Surely they could see the effort we were putting in? Yeah, the score doesn't show it, but that game really took it out of me and I know I wasn't the only one," he thought to himself, not wanting to roll over and face the headlines. "Can't lie in here all day, got to face them sometime today," he said to himself as he dragged himself from under the warm blankets.

"JUNIOR BOYS FORGET TO COME OUT FOR SECOND HALF!"

He looked at the headline and knew this wasn't going to be pretty.

All Kings junior side must have forgotten that rugby is played over two halves when they forgot to

*come out and play for the second
half in yesterday's whitewash at
Westchester.*

"Ouch!" Bootsie thought to himself as
he continued to read the paper.

*The superior Westchester forward
pack left a bruised and battered All
Kings team in its shadows as they ran
rampant over a tired and helpless All
Kings side. Things looked promising at
the half time break with neither team
being able to put points on the board.
What was set up for a cracking second
half quickly turned into a display of
soft and weak defending by the All
Kings team, allowing Westchester to
embarrass the junior side into a 60 to
0 final score.*

*Thankfully the senior boys redeemed
the school's name by crushing the
Westchester senior side 12 to 5. More*

on the senior boys crushing win in the sport section. Hopefully next week not only Socks will be pulling up his socks and putting in a better effort. Remember John, Bootsie and the rest of you junior boys, there are two halves in a game and you should play the full two halves each week. To sum up in one word PATHETIC!!

Bootsie could feel his internal temperature rising to an all new level. "This is too much," he said to himself as he tried to control his anger. "Superior Westchester forward pack. Were they even watching the same game that I played in? Senior boys' crushing win. They only won by seven points. Who writes this garbage?" he thought to himself. He threw the paper onto his desk and headed for the dining hall for breakfast. He sat down next to Razzi, John and the rest of the junior boys team who were all together at one table.

"Can you feel the heat from all the evil stares?" Razzi joked to the rest of the table as he looked around the dining hall.

"How can you joke about the garbage they write about us?" asked an unimpressed Bootsie.

"Look at them sitting over there," said Razzi as he looked over at the table where most of the papers contributors sat. "Soft, all of them," he snarled as he stared at the group who were in hot discussion about something.

"Soft you say, you mean soft like the Westchester boys? If they were so soft why am I so sore?" asked a frustrated Bootsie.

"Softer then," replied Razzi.

"Forget the paper, Bootsie, it means nothing. Do you think any of them could play any better, I mean look at them," said John, the team's captain, as he tried to calm an angry Bootsie. Bootsie didn't just look at them he stared at them, and if his eyes were lasers he would have burned holes in them.

After breakfast, Bootsie went to the office where the paper was put together. The All Kings Gazette was produced in an empty classroom-turned-office by a group of students who were hoping to be future journalists or reporters, either in TV or for the papers. The paper was well set up and had its own printing machines.

When he charged into the room most of the boy journalists were either sitting around praising their latest work or busily typing for the next edition of the paper.
"Don't let them get to you," were the words that were holding Bootsie back

from unleashing his thoughts on what felt like his new enemies before him. "If you explode now, you'll cop it from them for the rest of the year," was also going through his head as he stood there with every eye in the room now staring at him, waiting for him to say what he had come in for.

"Walk away, walk away, and say nothing," he silently said to himself over and over.

"Did you want something?" asked one of the boys just to break the silence.

"Um, yes. I didn't get a copy of the paper yet," was all Bootsie could think of, as he started to backpedal away from the reason he had really gone in there.

"There's a pile of them over there," the boy added as he pointed to the stack of unread papers.

"Oh' thanks. I'll just grab one then," added Bootsie as he walked over and picked one off the top of the pile and left without a confrontation.

"Damn it," he said to himself as he got outside and away from earshot of the boy journalists.

"Still letting them get to you?" said a voice. Bootsie looked up and saw his coach leaning on a wall nearby, reading his copy of the latest paper.

"They just print such..." Bootsie tried to say.

"Rubbish?" asked his coach. "It's their opinion that's all, it doesn't mean its true just because they think it or write it," he added.

"But people read it and believe it," said a still angry Bootsie.

"People read it and the next day it's forgotten about," added his coach, "Next week it'll be something else and the week after that something else. You've just got to rise above it, or it will eat at you until you start believing what they write is true, and that's when it really affects your game. I've seen some of the finest talent go to waste because of it. If you can learn to rise above this stuff *now* and you can make it to Test level, I can almost guarantee you that one day you'll be saying exactly the same thing to one of your teammates when he reads a negative comment about *his* name in the paper," said his coach as he looked down at Bootsie. He handed Bootsie his paper.

"Here, take this it's yours," said his coach as he handed a baffled Bootsie his copy of the paper.

"I've already got one," replied Bootsie as he showed him his own copy. "Just incase you need extra toilet paper," his coach laughed. "Rise above it," he added as he walked away.

Once again Bootsie's coach had straightened him out. He walked back to the dormitories and thought about what the coach had just told him. "The guy is a Regional and Test legend and on top of that he gives the best advice and always knows exactly what I am feeling. He's been in my shoes, he's been through this himself and he rose above it all to become the legend he is. Imagine if he had let it get to him and he had crumbled, the Region and Country would have missed out on one of the greatest players ever to pull on a boot."

Bootsie returned to his dormitory and lay on his bed. He looked at the paper and thought, "That's the last time you will make me feel this way. I'm bigger and better than this and never again will you make me feel like I'm not good enough to play this game here. Next week you'll be writing different headlines. You wait and see." Bootsie was right about one thing, the following week the paper would be writing different headlines, but unfortunately for him he just didn't know it would get even worse before it ever got better.

4

Saint Benedicts College

1912
Dei gratia

Rugby Union

The Red V

At training during the week, the coach really took it easy on the junior boys. He knew they had given it their all against Westchester and punishing them at training this week wasn't going to help anyone. The boys played a game of touch rugby at training but when a player was touched he had to go to ground and other players had to arrive, support the player on the ground and form a ruck over him. Bootsie felt a lot better after the light session and felt like he had recovered enough to play against Saint Benedict's on Saturday. He noticed in the Thursday edition of The Gazette that Saint Benedicts had four wins from four games and were still second on the ladder.

Junior Boys Ladder – Week 4

	P	W	L	D	B	F	A	Pts
Westchester College	4	4	0	0	4	180	37	20
Saint Benedicts	4	4	0	0	3	129	38	19
All Kings	4	3	1	0	1	52	70	13
St Josephs	4	2	2	0	1	59	67	9
St Mark's	4	2	2	0	1	65	112	9
Christian Boys	4	2	2	0	0	42	67	8
St Luke's	4	1	2	0	2	76	112	6
St Peter's	4	1	3	0	1	79	93	5
St David's	4	0	4	0	4	58	76	4
Bluedale College	4	0	4	0	2	48	116	2

All Kings were away again to Saint Benedicts, another school that loved its rugby. The school was built in 1912 and their Latin motto was *Dei gratia* which means 'by the grace of God', and their school colours were red and white. Although the Southern Region's jumpers were red and white stripes, when Bootsie ran out onto the field and saw the jumpers and colours of Saint Benedicts he felt like he was playing against the old enemy again. The Saint Benedict's team wore white jumpers with a big red V on the front, white shorts and red and white striped socks. By the end the day Bootsie would soon learn he hated the red V as much as the red and white stripes of the Southern Region.

Saint Benedicts had four wins from four games and it was for a good reason. They were good. For the entire first half Bootsie and the rest of the junior All Kings boys were behind. They were behind in everything including the score. The two previous games had really taken it out of the team, especially the previous week's game against Westchester College.

Bootsie's legs were good for the first thirty minutes but towards the end of the half he was a good ten metres behind the Saint Benedicts boys. This reminded him of his first training sessions with the Hornets, the problem today was this was happening *during* a game. By the end of the first half the score was Saint Benedicts 21, All Kings 0.

"What's happened to you boys?" asked the coach who was at a loss to work out the team's problems. "Surely you're not burnt out already?" The coach looked at the team's captain and asked, "Is that the problem John? Are you boys burnt out already? Surely that can't be it."

"No Coach. We'll get out there and show them what we're made of in the second half," replied John who looked a little exhausted himself. Bootsie didn't think *he* was burnt out, but maybe the pressure of the goldfish bowl environment he was living in and the press *was* actually getting to him. His coach had told him he had seen it make good players play worse, when they let it get to them.

"Surely it's not getting to me," Bootsie had to ask himself. "Why am I even thinking about it then. Oh no, maybe it *is* getting to me. Well I'll show them in this half that it's *not* getting to me," he said to himself, as he stood on the field and waited for the referee to blow his whistle. "Pheew!" The whistle sounded and the second half was underway.

Bootsie looked up at the high ball from the kick off sail towards him, as he looked up at the incoming ball he glanced at the crowd and could see the boy reporters in a group looking at him. His eyes became fixed on them for a split second, and in that split second the ball slowed in the wind and dropped suddenly. Bootsie looked up, and the ball hit him smack in the face.

"Ouch!" he said to himself as he put his face in his hands. He could feel the warmth of his blood filling his cupped hands as he held his face and nose. As he pulled his face out from his bloodied hands he could see all the boy reporters were busily writing in their notebooks.

"There's a headline," Bootsie said to himself, as he was led off the field.

"He can't come back on until the bleeding stops. You've got fifteen minutes to stop it, or his replacement will become permanent," said the referee to Bootsie and his coach.

"C'mon let's go get you cleaned up," said his coach to Bootsie.

As Bootsie sat in the change rooms, his coach said what he was already thinking.

"They've got to you again, haven't they?" he asked.

"Is it that obvious?" replied Bootsie. "I just saw them standing there talking and I froze, because I knew for sure they were talking about me," he added.

"They were probably talking about what was for dinner or some other stupid thing," replied his coach.

"But they started to write in their notebooks as soon as I dropped the ball," said Bootsie.

"That's because you gave them something to write about. Scoring tries and playing like a machine. Let them write about *that*. If you go out there and give it everything you've got and they still write rubbish about you, then it's their problem not yours," replied his coach.

"I did that last week and they still wrote bad things about us," said Bootsie, as he held his bloodied nose. "Yeah, and you listened to it. Shame on you I say," replied his coach as he wiped his hands on a now bloodied white towel. "The bleeding's finally stopped and I think we've still got time to get you back out there. Now go out there and give the press something to *really* write about," added his coach, as he led Bootsie out of the change room and towards the field.

Luckily Bootsie made it back onto the field after fourteen minutes and thirty seconds and the referee allowed him back on the ground. During the time he was down in the change rooms, All Kings had scored twice and the score was All Kings 14, Saint Benedicts 21. There is a term used in sport when a ball hits you anywhere in the head including the face, it is called a Falcon. From the moment Bootsie ran out onto the field again, he was the Falcon. "FALCON, FALCON, FALCON," the crowd shouted at him, and it was coming from *both* sides of the field! Bootsie had heard of the name but wasn't ready to be called it during *this* game or *any* game.

He desperately tried to redeem himself in the second half; he tried to make his tired body keep up with the action, but it was failing. He was still putting his body on the line at any breakdown he could get to, but he just wasn't fast enough to get to many of them. One of the Saint Benedict's players gave away a penalty for backchat and the All Kings fly half did his job and put the ball over the cross bar, All Kings 17, Saint Benedicts 21.

The game was locked at this score until very late into the game. The ball was being kicked from one full back to the other, and Bootsie found himself inside the Saint Benedicts half but had to retire towards his own kicker as he was offside under the ten metre law. As he jogged back, the All Kings full back, Freddy, booted the ball back up the field and was chasing his own kick. Freddy sprinted past Bootsie and as he went past, Bootsie knew he was back onside and began to run after him towards the ball.

It was an ugly ball for the defending player waiting to catch, as the sun was in his eyes and he was blinded by it. He had to let it bounce on the ground before he could even see it. It was a terrible bounce too; it went straight back five metres to the charging Freddy, who had now made it up to where the ball had landed. He took the ball on his chest and headed towards the line with Bootsie hotly following in support. Freddy had one boy in defence to beat, the left-winger, who was all alone defending his line and his own teammates were furiously trying to get back to help him. The winger had to do what any good defender in his situation should do. Stay wide and not come inside the field and not tackle the ball carrier unless there was no other option.

Unfortunately his support didn't arrive and he had to run infield to tackle the ball carrier, this left Bootsie wide open on the wing. It was a terrible pass that went above Bootsie's head, and as he reached up to grab it he felt it whiz straight through his fingertips. Bootsie quickly turned around and watched his dreams of glory roll up and over the touchline out of play.

"That's *time* boys," said the referee as he blew his whistle. Bootsie put his hands on his head; he couldn't believe what had just happened.

"Sorry Bootsie. I'm sure that pass will make the headlines tomorrow," Freddy joked, as he patted Bootsie's back. Final score All Kings 17, Saint Benedicts 21.

5

Sunday Edition

The All Kin

FALCON TO BLAME FOR

Our junior boys sank to all
new depths on the ladder
after a woeful display of
rugby skills from a certain
player yesterday. We had a
poor start to the game but
it got better when our
supposed first scholarship
choice left the field early in
the second half. When our
waste of a scholarship
Bootsis the Falcon came
back onto the field the
team suffered once again.
There was a golden
opportunity to win the
game by the Falcon in the
dying stages of the game
when he received an easy
pass from the fullback
Freddy but our supposed

star player blew it big time.

Luckily our senior boys are
holding up the flag for the
school and had a
comfortable 3 point win
over the senior Saint
Benedict boys, more on
their win in the sport
section at the back. How
much worse can it get? Do
we have to endure another
similar performance this
week to find out? Surely
the coach has to do
something about this; after
all he is the one who
continually puts him on
the field. Stay tuned to the
Gazette to find out more.

Ren
foll
imp

The
that
rela
the
beh
of a
exp
in h
its
beh
con
or v

It m
tota
thin
dec:

Faith

As Bootsie lay in his bed early on Sunday morning he was fearful of what would be written in the paper.

"Surely I'm not going to be blamed for that loss; surely Freddy's pass is going to take the heat away from me this week." These were the thoughts going through Bootsie's mind as he hid from the world under his blankets. He peeked out at his wardrobe door, the usual place the paper was pinned on a Sunday morning and could read the headline from where he lay.

FALCON TO BLAME FOR SHOCKER!!

"Are you kidding me?" he asked himself. He jumped out of bed to read the rest of the report.

Our junior boys sank to all new depths on the ladder after a woeful display of rugby skills from a certain player yesterday. We had a poor start to the game but it got better when our supposed first scholarship choice left the field early in the second half. When our waste of a scholarship Bootsie 'the Falcon' came back onto the field the team suffered once again. There was a golden opportunity to win the game by the Falcon in the dying stages of the game when he received an easy pass from the fullback Freddy, but our supposed star player blew it big time.

Luckily our senior boys are holding up the flag for the school and had a comfortable five point win over the senior Saint Benedict boys. More on their win in the sports section at the back. How much worse can it get? Do we have to endure another similar performance this week to find out? Surely the coach has to do something about this; after all he is the one who continually puts him on the field. Stay tuned to The Gazette to find out more.

"No, don't hold back, tell me what you really feel," Bootsie sarcastically said to himself as he read the paper. "I don't know whether to laugh or cry about it," he added. "A good pass from Freddy. Are they kidding? Even the coach is copping criticism this week; I don't think he'll like that," Bootsie thought as he threw the paper into the bin under his desk. For some reason even though it was the harshest criticism he had faced so far, it actually *didn't* bother him as much this week.

Although the criticism may not have bothered Bootsie, it certainly bothered someone else, the headmaster. He summoned Bootsie to be in his office late on Monday afternoon. Initially Bootsie was very worried about the conversation that might take place and when he saw the coach was also in the headmaster's office, his fears were heightened even more.

"How are things with you Bootsie?" asked the headmaster as Bootsie sat down.

"Well it seems every week but one so far, I have been front page news around here and not for the right reason either, but apart from that not bad," he replied in a very sarcastic voice. The headmaster laughed, "Yes you really are a talking point around here aren't you," he added as he sat down at his desk.

"Is that it; am I out of here now?" Bootsie asked the pair of them. He was surprised with the astonished looks he received from the coach and the headmaster.

"Of course not!" bellowed the head-master.

"Whoa Bootsie were not getting rid of you, we've got more faith in you than that," added his coach.

"I believe in freedom of the press and I've always let the paper print its stories regardless. The coach has told me how it's been getting to you a bit and now with the fact that the *coach* has been criticized, *you've* been criticized and even *I've* been criticized this week, we've decided to do something about it," said the headmaster.

"You've been criticized, where?" asked Bootsie.

"Right here," said the headmaster as he pointed to the first paragraph of the story. "Our waste of a scholarship choice," he said to Bootsie, "Who do you think made that choice? It was me. I can't be having my credit as a selector of scholarships threatened. I know your potential; the coach knows your potential. *You* just haven't played up to it yet and *we're* here to help you do that.

I know you are missing home and that's just something you'll get used to in your own time. In the meantime I've arranged for your parents to come down to watch this week's game. I've also asked your mum to bring a special pair of blue boots with her, I think you know the ones I mean?" he asked a very surprised Bootsie. Bootsie was so pleased to hear his family were coming down and bringing his Regional boots with them as well.

"Don't forget the other thing," the coach said to the headmaster.

"What other thing?" he replied with a curious look on his face.

"The paper, the special edition this week," added the coach.

"Oh yes of course," replied the headmaster, "Bootsie we need you to be extra keen at training this week, you know, be really fired up and show the other boys what you can do," added the headmaster to a slightly confused Bootsie.

"Um, Ok," was all he replied.

"You'll see. Don't worry," he said to Bootsie as he showed him out of his office. Bootsie returned back to the dormitory still scratching his head about the visit to the office. He *was* pleased to know he would see his parents and sister soon anyway.

Whilst Bootsie sat eating his breakfast on Thursday morning, there seemed to be a buzz going around the dining hall.

"Did you read the paper yet?" asked Razzi.

"No I think I'll give the paper a miss for a while," replied Bootsie.

"No you should really have a look. Here's mine," said Razzi as he threw Bootsie a copy of the paper. Bootsie opened the folded paper and was astonished at the headline on the front page, it read:

**Open tryouts tonight
everyone included.**

There will be open tryouts for every boy tonight in an attempt to regain form in the school's rugby team. We need some real men to step forward and save our beloved school from any further embarrassment and any further plunges on the ladder. All 1st, 2nd, and 3rd form boys will try out early in the afternoon and all 4th and 5th form boys will take part after the junior boys. ALL Students will attend with NO EXCUSES!! Any boy with an excuse MUST see the Headmaster.

"What's this all about?" Bootsie asked the boys at the table.

"Haven't got a clue," they replied,

"Word is, the boy journalists had a different story before it went to press last night, and when it came out this morning it had been changed. No one knows by who though," said Razzi.

"I think I do," Bootsie secretly thought to himself. "Extra keen at training this week," he also thought. "I think I know what might be going on here," he secretly chuckled as he ate his food.

Bootsie ran to training later that afternoon, he felt a whole new spring in his legs. The coach gathered the 1st, 2nd and 3rd form boys together in one massive group.

"Now this afternoon we will be playing a game and each of you will be rotated through the game to see if we've got any untapped talent we might have overlooked at All Kings. We'll start with some warm ups and go through some skills training before we get into the match," he said to the group as he looked over at Bootsie and smiled.

It was hilarious for Bootsie to watch his critics being put through their paces by the coach who he made sure they were nice and tired before the games began. For some reason Bootsie felt like he hadn't played a game all year and his legs were as fresh as daisies. Another strange thing to happen was at one point all the boy journalists somehow ended up on one team and the entire junior boy's team made up the other team.

"What are the odds of this happening?" Bootsie sneakily laughed to himself. He later learned a similar thing happened for the 4th and 5th form boys.

His coach came over to him and whispered, "Just give them a taste of the game, don't kill them," as he walked past. That's exactly what

Bootsie did. He gave all fifteen of the boy journalists on the other team just a small taste of what rugby was really like. Each time he put a tackle on one of them, he would reach out offering his hand to the poor soul still reeling on the ground, in an attempt to help him up and mend some damaged bridges. Would it work? Who knew, but it gave the boy journalists something to think about as they dragged their poor, tired and bruised egos back to the dormitories that afternoon.

6

Blue Boots

Words will never be able to describe the way Bootsie felt when he saw his parents and sister arrive at All Kings on that Saturday morning before his game. He had never ever been away from his family like this before. He quickly ushered his family to a quiet location before the full impact of seeing them again really hit him. He became very emotional and let a lot of tears out as he hugged both his parents; he was even very pleased to see his sister.

His mum had brought down the blue boots he'd received when he played in the two games for his region. All Kings had a strict *black boots only* rule that the headmaster was allowing to be broken just this once. Bootsie was so pleased to see his parents and wanted to tell them one hundred things at once.

"We've got all day and tomorrow dear. The school is letting us stay overnight in the guest quarters so you've got plenty of time to tell us everything," his mum said to a very excited Bootsie.

The headmaster came over to greet Bootsie's parents when he saw the four of them together.
"Welcome, welcome," he said as he greeted them with firm handshakes. He looked at Bootsie who had his blue boots hanging around his neck, "Is this why they call you Bootsie?" he laughed out loud to himself as he pointed at the boots around his neck. "That's actually the reason why," his mum grinned to a now surprised but still very happy headmaster. He looked down at his watch, "Bootsie hadn't you better, well, *be* somewhere? It's nearly time you know," added the headmaster.

"Oh yeah, the game," said Bootsie.

"We'll be in the grandstand, don't worry," added the headmaster as Bootsie took off towards the change rooms. The headmaster put on his All Kings cap and showed Bootsie's family down to the grandstand. It was packed with ex students all wearing their caps and the side of the field nearest the grandstand was a sea of green, black and yellow. The Saint Peter's crowd had also arrived and the other side of the field was awash with blue and white.

"My goodness, is it always like this?" asked a surprised Bootsie's mum.

"Always. I wish you could see it when St David's are here or we're over there. Madness it is," the headmaster replied.

When the junior boys ran out onto the field, the crowd was at its usual singing and chanting best.

"This is insane," his dad said as he leaned over to Bootsie's mum. "You're not wrong," she replied.

"What?" his dad asked pointing to his ears.

"I said you're not wrong," shouted his mum. His dad laughed as he motioned about the noise still coming from the crowd.

Bootsie was very used to the atmosphere by now, but for his parents it must have been like it was for him against Christian Boys College in his first game. When the referee came over and checked the studs on their boots, even he noticed Bootsie's blue boots.

"Regional boots, hey. Does your headmaster know you're wearing these today?" he asked Bootsie with a smile.

"Yeah, it's just a one off though," he replied.

"Ok then, but I've never seen it allowed here before," added the referee with a smile. He finished checking the studs, blew his whistle and the game was on.

Bootsie felt like a new boy as he stood waiting for the ball. He had been criticized until he should have cracked but hadn't, been the target of enough bad press to turn him away from the game but didn't and now with his parents in the stand, he was the first boy in the history of All Kings to be wearing something other than black boots. He knew with his blue boots on and parent's watching, something special was going to happen today. As the ball came down towards him he said goodbye to the Falcon, took the ball on his chest and ran up field.

It took four defenders to get him down at the first tackle. His legs didn't feel tired, his body felt good, he was refreshed and it was all because of the headmaster and coach. They had set up the front page of the paper and the tryouts where Bootsie got to extract sweet revenge on the boy journalists. They had also invited his family down to stay and allowed Bootsie to wear his blue boots which meant so much to him for this game. Bootsie knew how to repay them as well, on the field. He was on fire again; a spark that had almost gone out had been relit in him.

Bootsie's spark lit a fire under the rest of the junior boys as well. They all felt gloomy when anyone in the team was getting bad press, it reflected on *all* of them. They all had the greatest of respect for the coach and didn't like where they sat on the ladder at all. The poor St Peter's boys couldn't have picked a worse day to come to play at All Kings. They met a hard, fit and physical side and by half time the score was already All Kings 21, St Peter's 0.

"Finally, you boys are back!" said the coach at the break, "I've wondered where you all went in the last few weeks. Let's see if we can keep this up for the rest of the season and when the tourists get here on Monday," he added. The coach took the press with a grain of salt but even he didn't like where the All Kings junior boys sat on the ladder. He breathed a big sigh of relief as the boys took to the field for the start of the second half.

For the rest of the second half it was the 'blue-booted Bootsie show', he was back to his best and showing everyone why he had been selected on a full scholarship to this school in the first place. Tackling, hand offs, side steps, barging over and through defenders. He was doing it all. Halfway through the second half he had gained All Kings a four-try bonus point single handedly. Even John the captain was taking a back seat and letting him run the show for the day. He taught them the magnet move at a rest period for another injured St Peter's player and at the next breakdown, put big John the second rower through the massive gap that opened up before him. John the captain was in 3rd Form and knew that next year he would be fighting his way into the senior team. He now knew he had found his replacement captain for next season.

The Saint Peter's supporters were silenced from the very start of the game. They were seeing their boys massacred on the field by a very different team from the one they had faced last week. They were losing to a team that was not going to lose to anyone today. They were also being beaten by a boy in blue boots who was playing his heart out and finally silencing his many critics. Well, for this week anyway.

As Bootsie walked off the field after the game he looked over at the boy journalists who were once again gathered in a group. They could see just by looking at him, how much he had put in again today. Each and every one of them looked at and gave a nod of acknowledgement towards Bootsie. After the other night, they had been made to eat humble pie as well as the grass of the training field. Anyone could criticize and say they could do better, but until they actually got out there and tried it for themselves, they never knew. These boys had been forced into facing the truth, and the truth was just how hard rugby is.

Each of them had a new respect for the boys who took to the field each and every week and were then hammered by the press if *they* decided they hadn't played well enough. It had forced the boy journalists into the realization that they didn't have the skills or the courage to get out there and do better. It made the relationship between the players and the press better for everyone who ever attended All Kings College from that day forward. In the end the final score was All Kings 42, St Peter's 3.

7

Fortis est veritas
1
8
7
4

Charlton Hall

Rugby Union

The Tourists

During the fourteen round season of the competition, each team gets one weekend of rest with no game that weekend. For All Kings this weekend meant something completely different, tourists! And not the tourists that people would normally imagine.

The tourists were the visiting overseas team coming to All Kings for a game against the junior and senior sides.

They had stayed the previous week at Bluedale College, thrashing them 98 to 6 on the same Saturday that All Kings had beaten St Peter's. The bus from Bluedale College brought the team from Charlton Hall over to All Kings on Sunday evening instead of Monday morning as first planned. When Bootsie heard the score of the Charlton Hall vs. Bluedale game, he had to check again where Bluedale were on the ladder and which teams they had beaten this season. He flicked to the back of the paper and found the junior boys ladder for week 6.

Junior Boys Ladder – Week 6

	P	W	L	D	B	F	A	Pts
Saint Benedicts	6	5	1	0	3	171	90	23
Westchester College	6	4	2	0	5	212	78	21
All Kings	6	4	2	0	3	111	94	19
St Josephs	6	3	3	0	3	96	103	15
Christian Boys	5	3	2	0	1	77	88	13
St David's	6	2	4	0	4	86	94	12
St Mark's	5	2	3	0	1	72	127	9
St Peter's	6	2	4	0	1	101	153	9
St Luke's	5	1	3	0	3	94	131	7
Bluedale College	5	1	4	0	2	63	125	6

"Bluedale are on the bottom with only *one* win so far," he laughed to himself as he looked at the ladder. "One win," he laughed again.

"At least we're sitting in a more respectable spot this week," he said to himself as he noticed where All Kings were on the table.

"Saint Benedicts are still the team to beat, I wonder if we play them again this year?" he also thought to himself. Each week in the paper was a full copy of the season's fixtures and updated scores from each and every game. The boy journalists might be a critical bunch but when it came to things like this they really put in a good effort. Each week they would ring around and check each game's score and update the fixtures sheet accordingly. They would also update the ladder and print that in the same spot every week as well. Bootsie looked at the fixtures page for the end of week six.

He noticed in round five that Bluedale had beaten St Joseph's for their only win and St Joseph's were only one spot under All Kings on the ladder, and Charlton Hall had beaten Bluedale 98 to 6. He also noticed two last things before he put the paper away. One was that in round twelve they would face Saint Benedicts again and the other thing he noticed was in round fourteen. "Last round of the season, St David's at St David's, *nice*," he said to himself.

The boys from Charlton Hall were a great bunch of boys and blended into life at All Kings quite easily, they were on holiday so to speak and didn't have to attend any classes during the week. This gave them time to polish their skills on the rugby field. Each day they would train, *each* and *every* day that is. Bootsie spoke with a few of the boys and they were looking forward to the game on Saturday. They were quite proud about the thrashing they had given to Bluedale and told Bootsie as a tongue-in-cheek joke, to expect the same at All Kings. Bootsie smiled and laughed with them and showed them where Bluedale were on the ladder compared to All Kings, the rivalry was set up nicely for Saturday and Bootsie couldn't wait.

Finally game day arrived and Bootsie got to run out against the boys from Charlton Hall, it even sounded posh. For this day the All Kings jumpers were slightly different, the numbers on the back of the jumpers were in black instead of white. It was a tradition that at the end of any game whether at home or on tour to swap jumpers with the opposite numbered player on the other team. If in the future you ever saw an All Kings jumper with a black number on the back it meant it had been swapped either at home or during a visiting tour. "Another wacky All Kings tradition," Bootsie thought to himself when he was given his jumper.

The Charlton Hall boys ran out in their traditional red, white and blue colours. The jumpers were like the school flag, blue with a big red V on the front with a smaller white V on each side of the red V, blue shorts and blue, red and white striped socks. The school's emblem of white shield and blue cross was embroidered on the top left hand side of the jumper. Their school motto in Latin was *'Fortis est veritas'* which means 'Truth is strong'.

"We'll see how strong you boys are," Bootsie thought as the whistle was blown to start the match.

They might have been from a school with a reputation as one of the poshest and most prestigious schools in all of their country, but on the field they were an ugly team. From the opening whistle it was on, shoulder charges, studs being used in the rucks, high tackles with general rough and dirty play as well.

"So this was how you beat the boys at Bluedale was it?" Bootsie said to himself as he wiped some blood from his nose, the result of a high tackle. After the penalty kick at goal, it was All Kings 3, Charlton Hall 0.

Then the heavens opened and it poured down, the game became a sloppy, wet and *very* dirty affair. The All Kings boys were leaving the field in great numbers to be patched up and to stop bleeding wounds in general, and for the first half, the replacement players were seeing as much action as the starting fifteen. As each patched-up player came back onto the field he would usually swap with the replacement player who would now be bleeding from somewhere.

Bootsie loved playing in the wet. It had been a lot wetter where he had learned to play with the Bulldogs, but it didn't rain as much where the school was, so most of the All Kings boys fell apart in the wet conditions. The Charlton Hall boys were pretty good in the wet and this was reflected in the score at half time. All Kings 3, Charlton Hall 14.

"Boys don't let them keep up this sort of game and do nothing about it. Get out there and stand up for yourselves and the school. Physically stick it back to them, just keep it within the rules of the game, okay?" said the coach at half time, who wasn't happy about the supposed goodwill nature of the friendly inter-school game. His players had come into the dressing room like they had been in a losing battle, and they had another half to go yet.

As the boys sat in the change rooms they could hear how heavy the rain had got. It was absolutely pouring down out there. The gutters on the grandstand couldn't cope with the downpour and the water was flowing off the edges of the grandstand's roof like a curtain of water. It was soon hard to tell which team was which when the game restarted, the boys were so muddy it looked like thirty boys from one team were on the field. The Charlton Hall boys didn't let a bit of rain stop their rough house tactics in the second half either. The referee finally had enough and started dishing out yellow cards. The referee spoke to both captains and it actually fixed the problem. The game became a lot less dirty, in the rules of the game sense anyway, in the weather sense it was still filthy. Bootsie was pleased when he got a try late in the second half and he slid on the ground from just before the Charlton Hall five-metre line and let the wet ground do the rest. When Andy the All Kings fly half tried for the conversion, the ball was so wet and waterlogged he nearly broke his leg kicking it. The ball travelled about ten metres at head level and fell very short of the posts. By the end of the game Charlton Hall had won and the final score was Charlton Hall 19, All Kings 8. At least it was better than 98 to 6. The All Kings boys could feel very proud of the way they had played today.

8

South's Bulldogs

Rugby Union FC

Bootsie
The Bulldog

Finally, after being away from home for so long Bootsie was going home for the school holidays. He had been away for what seemed like forever and was now about to leave All Kings for two weeks and be with his family again. His parents had arranged to pick him up on the Sunday after the Charlton Hall game and then they were heading down to where they used to live to spend the two weeks at Bootsie's grandparent's house. His mum hadn't seen her parents since they had moved to the new town. Bootsie was pleased to spend time with his family no matter where they were staying; besides he too had missed his grandparents since the move.

Before he left All Kings he was told by the headmaster to rest up and be ready to come back in two weeks for the second and most important half of the season.

"We need you fighting fit and ready to win us the shield this season when you get back," said his headmaster.

"After yesterday's game I need all the rest I can get," replied Bootsie as he said his goodbyes to the headmaster. The private schoolboy competition took a two-week break over the school holidays and it would be a welcome relief for Bootsie, who had played in some very physical games already this year.

He spent the first week at his grandparent's house resting his tired young body, his grandmother really liked to fuss over him and although he normally didn't like it, for the first week anyway Bootsie really lapped it up. She would feed him a constant supply of homemade cakes and biscuits as he lazily sat around and watched TV. There was also a constant supply of Bootsie's relatives calling in to visit and he had to tell each one of them about All Kings over and over again. He didn't mind really, as they seemed so interested in knowing what it was like. Some of them were quite shocked when his mum told them about what the boy journalists were writing about him each week. Bootsie sent a copy of the All Kings Gazette home if he made the front page, so his mum had received quite a few editions of the paper over the last few weeks.

"It's all sorted now though," he told some of his relatives, as they listened in horror to his mum as she told them about the reports. "The headmaster and coach fixed that," he added.

"I should hope so," said one of his aunties.

Bootsie's holidays were speeding along and he hadn't really done anything, apart from watching a lot of TV. One day when his grandmother answered a knock at the door Bootsie recognised the voice at the front door.

"Wanna buy some chocolate old lady?" said the boy, "We're fundraising for our club," he added.

"Stinkey Taylor," Bootsie said to himself as he headed for the front door. He heard his grandmother giving the chocolate seller a good telling off for calling her an old lady.

"Where's your manners you rude little boy?" she scolded.

"Stinkey!" said Bootsie as he got to the door.

"Bootsie! What are you doing here?" asked Stinkey.

"This is my grandparent's house, we're down here for the holidays," replied Bootsie.

"Do you want some chocolates? We're fundraising for the Bulldogs," asked Stinkey.

"Can we get some?" asked Bootsie as he looked up at his still angry grandmother.

"Well only because of the team and not because of this rude young boy's manners or lack of them," she snapped back.

"What are you doing tomorrow?" Stinkey asked Bootsie.

"Nothing, I don't think anyway," replied Bootsie.

"Why don't you come down and play for the Bulldogs again? We need someone to fill in this week," asked Stinkey.

"I don't know if I should, I'll just ask my..."

"YES!" said Bootsie's mum who had been listening to the boys. "You've been sitting around here for nearly two weeks without moving. It will do you good," she added.

"Guess that settles it then," said Bootsie.

"It's a home game, starts at eleven. I'll see you down there," added a pleased Stinkey.

Bootsie thought the run would do him good and anyway all those biscuits and cakes weren't really what he should have been filling up on, if he wanted to keep his fitness level where it needed to be. Luckily he had his rugby gear from All Kings with him and would just have to play in his All Kings shorts and socks. As long as he had the Bulldogs jumper on it shouldn't cause too many problems. When they arrived at the ground the following morning Bootsie felt very strange. He always thought he was a Bulldog through and through, but when he stepped out of the car and onto the ground it didn't feel like home at all.

This hadn't been Bootsie's team for over two years now; he had played for the Hornets for two seasons, two games for the Region and now was playing for All Kings. The seasons at the Bulldogs now seemed like they were a lifetime ago. He met up with Stinkey and a few of the boys he used to play with as well. Sione, Sunnie, Ali and Tua still played but he found out Red and Ted had moved last year and didn't play for the Bulldogs anymore. Terry the terrier jumped on Bootsie's back when he saw Bootsie as he was so pleased to see him again.

Ben 'super boot' Smith was also pleased to see him and told him that he had been at the Regional camp and Robbie had told him about All Kings. Bootsie was just pleased to hear that

Robbie had even gone to the camp after telling Bootsie he didn't think he would ever play again. He was pleased to hear that Robbie had been selected to play for the Region again, poor Ben had missed out because of it though, so Bootsie had some very mixed feelings about it.

"You're back!" someone said as Bootsie felt a large pair of hands on his shoulders. He quickly turned around to see who had cast the large shadow over him.

"Coach Van Den!" he said excitedly when he looked up.

"Good to see you in Bulldogs colours again, although what's going on with the socks and shorts? Is it a fashion statement or something?" he asked Bootsie with a smile.

"No, Stinkey said you guys needed some extra players this week so I came down. I'm down here on holidays from

All Kings," Bootsie replied.

"Yes we all heard about the scholarship, Ben filled us in after he got back from camp," said Coach Van Den, "We were all very pleased when we heard the news," he added. "Poor young Ben tried out two years in a row and missed both times," continued the coach.

"Yeah, I know the boy who plays fly half, he lives in my street and we used to play on the same club team before I went to All Kings," he replied, "He's a great player," Bootsie added.

"Are you still coaching this team?" asked Bootsie who couldn't work out why all the boys had their jumpers on before the coach had arrived. "No, just for this week. I don't know why this competition still runs during the holidays it seems a little strange. Their coach has gone away for the week and his son plays on the team so you'll be taking his spot. I've spoken to your mum and she was more than happy for you to play," said Coach Van Den. "I think she's just happy I got out of the house for a bit," replied Bootsie.

When Bootsie stood on the field waiting for the start of the game he really felt out of place, he must have looked quite strange wearing a red, green and white bulldog's jumper with black shorts and green, black and yellow striped socks plus the blue boots.
"Oh well it's only one game," he thought to himself as the referee finally blew his whistle. Bootsie was soon amazed at either how fast he was or how slow the game was, whatever it was he felt like he was playing against younger boys.

They were playing their old rivals the South East Cats and none of their players were able to stop Bootsie when he had the ball in hand. Each time he took off up field he kept finding himself with no support and kept getting penalised for not releasing the ball in a tackle. At the half time break the other boys looked slightly exhausted but Bootsie felt fine. He had even been sitting around for the last two weeks eating biscuits and hadn't trained once. Coach Van Den was impressed.

"Is it the air up where you live now or something?" he asked Bootsie. "You're killing them out there. Good work," he added.

"Big hills," was all Bootsie replied with a smile.

The second half was much the same as the first, Bootsie charging through boys like they were made of butter. He scored two solo effort trys in the first half and two more early in the second half. He put Sunnie and Sione both over for a try each as well. Late in the second half the score was Bulldogs 42, South East Cats 7. At least he was enjoying the game, especially when he heard some of the Cats players complaining that he was too good for this competition as he was a Regional player. Bootsie didn't like to brag at all. It wasn't in his nature but even *he* had to admit, it did make him feel a bit special.

He felt great at least until late in the game when his leg got stuck in a ruck and he heard a sound like "CRACK!" "Aagh my ankle!" he screamed as the pile of bodies picked themselves of him. Coach Van Den helped him off the field and over to his parents. His dad tried to take off his boot. "Aagh that hurts," said Bootsie.

"Looks a bit purple already," said Coach Van Den, "Hopefully it's just a sprain," he added.

"Come on son we'd better take you to the hospital for an x-ray," said his dad.

"It was good to see you again anyway Bootsie," said Coach Van Den as he helped Bootsie take off his Bulldogs jumper.

"See you Bootsie," all the Bulldogs players shouted as they saw him limp away from the field with his dad holding him up. Bootsie didn't say anything and just waved back. He was in too much pain. When he thought about what the headmaster at All Kings was going to say about his injury, his ankle hurt even more.

9

Spectator

The Sunday after the game with the Bulldogs was the day Bootsie had to return to All Kings. His parents dropped him off at the school on the way through to them returning home from their holiday as well. It was late on Sunday evening when they arrived at the school and they still had quite a trip ahead of them before they got home. Bootsie's dad carried his suitcase into his dormitory for him whilst Bootsie limped alongside him with the help of his crutches. They were met by Syd just outside the dormitory.

"Oh dear what has happened to you my boy?" he asked Bootsie in his thick Indian accent.

"It's just a sprain, nothing broken," replied his dad.

"Here let me help you," said Syd, as he held the door open for Bootsie and his dad to go through.

After making sure that Bootsie was comfortable, his dad gave him a hug and turned to leave. "Remember if you need anything, just ring," he said to Bootsie as he waved goodbye.

The news of Bootsie's injury spread fast in the goldfish bowl. He must have explained to twenty different boys how it happened.

"How long will you be out for?" asked one boy.

"Four to six weeks they said," replied Bootsie.

"Ooh that's nearly the season, the headmaster's not going to like this when he hears about it," continued the boy.

"Don't worry, I'm not looking forward to telling him either," replied a very worried Bootsie.

"Maybe you should make something up, tell him you were skateboarding or something," said another boy.

"No I'll just stick with the truth. I'm terrible at lying anyway, I'd rather just be honest about it," replied Bootsie.

It was just as well for Bootsie he was honest because when he was summoned to the headmaster's office early on Monday morning he was already aware of how the injury had happened.

"Bootsie, Bootsie," he said as he paced his office with his hands behind his back, "Why were you playing for another team in the first place? That's what I can't get over. You're at All Kings now, and you should only be playing for All Kings. Didn't I tell you to rest before you left? Out there, I specifically remember telling you before you left you were to rest and come back ready to help us win the shield, remember?" added the headmaster. Bootsie could tell by the tone in his voice he wasn't impressed at all with what had happened to him.

"I'm lost for words Bootsie, you were the key to us winning the shield this season, I know it. And now you're out for how long? Five, maybe six weeks, that's the season gone!" he said to Bootsie.

"I was hoping maybe three to four weeks, which means I could still play in some of the games," replied Bootsie trying to make the situation sound better.

"Well I just hope your team mates can keep winning and give us some chance of being at the top of the table, if and when you can come back and play," he added, as Bootsie just sat there and listened to what he was saying, not being able to change anything about the situation he was in. He didn't want to say it was just an accident even though it was, he didn't think it was what the headmaster wanted to hear right at *this* moment.

This week All Kings were away at St Luke's, Bootsie thought they were bottom of the ladder and waited until the Thursday edition of The Gazette to check the current table. Bootsie was amazed to see some of the changes in the ladder; he quickly turned to the fixtures page to see why there had been so many changes and why All Kings hadn't moved in the week they hadn't played.

Junior Boys Ladder, Week 7.

	P	W	L	D	B	F	A	Pts
Saint Benedicts	7	5	2	0	3	176	105	23
Westchester College	6	4	2	0	5	212	78	21
All Kings	6	4	2	0	3	111	94	19
Christian Boys	6	4	2	0	1	82	91	17
St David's	7	3	4	0	4	103	106	16
St Josephs	7	3	4	0	4	108	120	16
St Peter's	7	3	4	0	1	116	158	13
Bluedale College	6	2	4	0	2	75	132	10
St Mark's	6	2	4	0	2	79	139	10
St Luke's	6	1	4	0	3	97	146	7

"Wow St Peter's beat Saint Benedicts, and I see Westchester had their week off as well so mainly only the bottom sides have moved around, no wonder it looks so different," he said to himself. One thing he did notice was the race for the top spot was now being contested by six teams and any one of these teams were in a position to get to the top over the coming weeks.

"If we can keep winning for the next few weeks, hopefully I can get back and we can still be in with a chance of winning the shield," he thought to himself.

When all fourteen rounds of the competition are finished, the team on top of the ladder wins the 'Skelton Shield' and gets to keep it in their school's trophy cabinet until the following year. The huge shield, contested for since 1921 is covered in miniature silver shields, each engraved with the name of the winning school and the year.

At training Bootsie sat in the stand and watched his teammates run around.

He would have to get used to sitting in the grandstand over the next five weeks. The All Kings boys thrashed St Luke's on the Saturday and it certainly made Bootsie a lot more comfortable around the headmaster. He could only imagine what would happen if the boys lost every game whilst he sat and watched their chances of the shield sitting in the All Kings trophy cabinet, slip away.

By the end of the five weeks Bootsie was quite pleased with how the boys had done without him, and at one point he wondered if they even needed him at all. They had only lost one game out of the last five. Of course the press had a bit to say on the matter, but it was a small article in the back of the paper and wasn't overly personal. It was supposed to be an article about Bootsie returning to the team in round thirteen and how they really hadn't missed him but due to other boys being injured they *would* need him this week. "We don't need you but we do need you, doesn't make a lot of sense," he thought to himself as he read the article. He made a sterling comeback against St Luke's in round 13 but unfortunately the injury-plagued All Kings boys went down at home. The final score was St Luke's 21, All Kings 7.

The Sunday morning after the game was the first time Bootsie had ever stood outside the office where The Gazette was put together and waited for the paper. The boy journalists had stayed up all night compiling the paper with the last updated ladder and fixtures before the final game of the season. At dawn on Sunday morning the paper was finished and ready for delivery to the dormitories.

As the door of the office opened Bootsie grabbed his copy from the top of the pile on the delivery trolley. "No need to pin one to my wardrobe door this week, I'll just take mine now," he said to a very startled journalist who he had taken by surprise.

"Its front page news" he said to Bootsie as he walked off with his trolley full of papers. Bootsie looked at the headline.

Skelton Shield comes down to a thriller!!

Bootsie quickly read the article.

The Skelton Shield is building up to a thrilling final game next week. All Kings may have the shield within their grasp, but they need to win and get a bonus point victory as well as deny St David's a losing bonus point before they could clinch the title for this season. The game is at St David's so they have the home advantage, and it will take everything our injury-ravaged team has got to pull this off. We welcomed back our scholarship hero last week after his injury scare and he was the only shining light for the team, scoring our only try. More on this thrilling game in the sport section and there will be a sports special in Thursday's edition dedicated to the gripping game.

Bootsie could hardly believe his eyes. This was the first good press he'd had for the way he'd played in a match that they had *lost*.

Things *had* changed. He looked at the table printed on the front page of the paper.

Junior Boys Ladder – Week 13

	P	W	L	D	B	F	A	Pts
St David's	12	8	4	0	6	204	158	38
All Kings	12	7	5	0	6	240	166	34
Saint Benedicts	12	7	5	0	4	276	198	32
Westchester College	12	7	5	0	4	327	202	32
St Josephs	12	6	6	0	6	159	188	30
Bluedale College	12	5	7	0	6	202	218	26
Christian Boys	12	5	7	0	4	175	200	24
St Peter's	12	6	6	0	3	200	274	23
St Mark's	12	4	8	0	5	166	236	21
St Luke's	12	4	8	0	3	168	297	19

"Yep they're right, it's going to be a thriller next week that's for sure," he thought to himself after looking at the ladder.

10

It's Going To
Be A Thriller

The boy journalists had done their research, it was a two-horse race to the finish and All Kings could win the shield with a bonus point victory but they also had to deny St David's getting a losing bonus point, by ensuring that they beat them by more than seven points. If All Kings won without the bonus point it would be a tie and they would have to play again the following week. If the boys could pull off the win, the four-try bonus point *and* deny St David's the losing bonus point, the Skelton Shield would be in the trophy cabinet of All Kings once again. This game was going to be good.

At training during the week the players looked like the walking wounded. There was more tape, bandages and strapping on the boys than Bootsie had ever seen before. Bootsie only hoped that by Saturday things would get better and some of the injured boys could make it through a full game. The coach was very easy on the boys, there was no point at all in pushing anyone and they all just walked around the training ground as he spoke and told the group about big games he had played in. The boys lapped it up.

Saturday morning soon arrived and Bootsie was full of pre match nerves as he travelled on the bus to St David's. It was a big one for him and he knew the whole school was looking at him and he was expected to perform. He wasn't stupid, he knew why he was given the scholarship, he knew it didn't matter what he scored on the aptitude test, he knew why the headmaster had selected him and it was for one reason. Days like TODAY!!

The dressing rooms at St David's were built underneath the grandstand, and in the All Kings room it looked like a first-aid clinic. Some of the boys looked like Egyptian mummies they had so many bandages on them. It had been a tough thirteen weeks for them including the Charlton Hall game. The only good thing about Bootsie and *his* injury was that he was in better shape than most of the other junior boys were. He had only played one game in the last six weeks and although not as fit as he would have liked to have been, he was in good physical shape and his ankle was now pretty good. It was time for his coach to address his troops for the last time.

"The way I see it boys, is we have got to go all out this week and win with the four-try bonus point, anything else is just too risky. If we lose, its curtains, if we win without the bonus point it's on again next week and I don't think your injuries will make it through another week. If we don't smash them today and they get a losing bonus point they're going to win anyway. We've got no choice but to go for the lot this week, I know some of you are hurting but if you can give me one more big game it'll all be over and victory will take away the pain from your injuries," he said to the group. It fired the boys up and when they ran out of the dressing room and up the ramp onto the field they were pumped for a big game.

Bootsie stood on the field and looked at the huge crowd that had gathered to watch the game. It was without doubt the biggest crowd he had ever played in front of. Spectators from every private school in the competition were there, and with the usual massive St David's home crowd and the extra number of All Kings supporters it was an enclosed field with not a single gap anywhere outside the field of play.

"Just blow the whistle before I have to run to the toilet," he thought to himself as he stood there shaking with nerves.

"Green captain are you ready? Black captain are you ready?" asked the referee. "Pheew!" he blew his whistle and it was on.

The intensity of the opening five minutes was incredible, it was no place for the weak and if you weren't going in hard you were going to get hurt. Bootsie felt like he had lost his hearing but he knew it was just the massive noise coming from the enormous crowd. For the opening twenty minutes he was on fire, it was tough as nails out on the field and he was the hammer. He was hard at the ball, hard at the tackle and hard at the breakdown, what a day for everything to fall into place for him. His body felt good, but his ankle was a slightly different story.

Although he was playing in pain he made sure he led by example. Unfortunately for All Kings he was in the minority, the other boys had played five more games in this competition than he had and it was showing. He couldn't be mad about that, it wasn't fair but he could be mad that some of them seemed to have quit already. When St David's got two easy trys before the second half Bootsie was furious. He knew the difference between a pulled muscle and a pulled heart muscle; some of the All Kings players had strained their heart muscles. The half time score was All Kings 5, St David's 14.

He sat in the dressing room and looked around at the group; most of the boys had their heads down and looked beaten. Even though they had played more games than he had, he knew they had more in them than they had showed so far in the first half. Bootsie had to lead from the front and this was the time to do it. He pulled off his boot and threw it at the wall; it certainly got everyone's attention. He pulled down his sock to reveal a very swollen, black and purple ankle.

"Look at this!" he shouted, "My ankle's not better. It's killing me. I rolled it again running up the ramp before the start of the game. But do you think its going to stop me today? NO! It's not. Now I know you're hurting but if you think you're in pain then how do you think I'm feeling?" he asked the group.

Now looking back, it was probably the pain he was in, making him act a bit crazy but Bootsie shouted at the group, "DON'T EVEN GO BACK OUT THERE IF YOU'RE NOT PREPARED TO GIVE IT EVERYTHING YOU'VE GOT. LOSING ISN'T AN OPTION TODAY!!" The rev-up worked too; the shocked boys all stood up as one and stood in a circle, they put their hands in the middle as one and shouted ALL KINGS!! They ran onto the field with a whole new attitude.

"Great speech," the coach said to Bootsie, who was trying to get his boot on over his swollen ankle. "I can't let you play on that!" he told Bootsie.

"Just strap it and I mean heavy. It's not going to keep me out of the next war or anything," replied a fired-up Bootsie. The coach knew no matter what he said to him, Bootsie would take the field, so he strapped it as best he could to get him out there.

Every step he took on his ankle was like stepping on a nail, the pain shot right up his leg, but as the second half started and the adrenaline started to run through his body again, the pain became almost bearable. He was like a true general, leading from the front. "Don't ask others to do what you're not prepared to do yourself," he said to himself as he chased and tackled a St David's defender. It was like being a roman gladiator in a coliseum; every move on the field was followed by a roar from the crowd. For some reason it seemed like every other school was shouting for the All Kings players while only St David's supporters were shouting for their own team. Bootsie took the ball off the back of the scrum and barged over the line for the second All Kings try. With a missed conversion from Andy, the score was All Kings 10, St David's 14.

The action became furious again straight after the try. There was a lot riding on the result of this game. The rivalry between the teams was fierce and went back many years. St David's changed their strategy and started the dirty tactics again. Bootsie and his teammates were being covered in marks from the St David's players' boot-studs being illegally used in the rucks. The referee was missing half of it, as it seemed they were using the most unfit referee they could find and he was never near the action. Bootsie was kicked, stomped on and high-tackled and he wasn't alone. The sideline became a casualty ward and the coach was the doctor. The boys picked and drove the ball over 21 phases to get the ball up to the St David's goal line. Bootsie yelled at John to come to the back of the ruck and pick up the ball, and as he did so, Bootsie grabbed him by his jumper and they both crashed over the line and John got the ball down. Andy had to take the conversion kick right next to the St David's supporters and missed the goals completely. All Kings 15, St David's 14.

The game had come down to the last few minutes and it was a brutal display of the game they say is played in heaven. Bootsie took the ball from a great pass and found himself in a gap, he was through and the try line was getting closer. The last two defenders both went for Bootsie, it left Andy running next to him with no defender to beat, he passed the ball to him and Andy dived over the line for the try.

"Pheew! TRY! The grounding's fine," shouted the referee. The score was All Kings 20, St David's 14.

"Once the kick is made, the game's over," said the referee.

"What?" asked Bootsie.

"The siren's already gone. Didn't you hear it?" asked the referee.

"NO," he replied.

"No pressure Andy, if you make the kick we win the season, and if you *miss*, St David's will get a losing bonus point and we'll both be on 39 points and have to play again next week," Bootsie thought to himself as he walked over to Andy, who for some reason was still on the ground with the coach leaning over him.

"He's out cold," said the coach, "The dirty St David's defender kneed him in the head as he scored. Someone else has to take the kick," he added as he lifted a semi-conscious Andy to his feet.

"B... B... Bootsie can do it, I've seen him kick at training," he said in a very groggy voice.

"Make a decision," said his coach to John, the team's captain, as he started to walk to the sideline with Andy.

"You've got one minute," said the referee. Now Bootsie didn't know exactly how many people were at the game that day but when John handed *him* the kicking tee the whole crowd was going crazy.

"Haven't we got anyone else who can take the kick?" Bootsie asked his captain.

"I wouldn't have given the tee to anyone else, I've got faith in *you* Bootsie, *you* are the right person to take the kick," John replied as he patted Bootsie on his back before leaving him to take the kick.

As Bootsie lined up the ball he knew he would have to kick with his sore ankle, there was no way he would be able to put all his weight on it if he used it as his support leg. For some bizarre reason a silence fell over the crowd, which was a first during a game of private schoolboys' rugby. Bootsie stepped back from the tee four paces and out five paces to his right, he stood and looked at the posts for as long as he could before dropping his gaze to the ball. He knew that on top of everything this was going to hurt, no matter what. He approached the ball and "WOOMF" kicked it as hard as he could, he just wasn't ready for how much it *would* hurt.

"AAAGH!!" he screamed as he fell to the ground. He rolled over to watch the ball heading towards the posts and then it all went black.

The pain was so intense that Bootsie passed out, and the next thing he knew he was on a stretcher being carried off the field. He looked up at the sky while his body bounced painfully as he was carried along the field towards the changing rooms. Was he a hero, had his kick been successful? The sky was soon replaced by the concrete roof leading into the changing rooms. The sound of the crowd disappeared, and he heard a familiar voice. "You're a hero son, a true hero. People are going to talk about you and this game forever," the voice said. He looked up and could see his headmaster leaning over him and smiling. Bootsie had made the kick, his first-ever attempt at a conversion in a game and it had won the Skelton Shield. He had cemented his place in All Kings history in his first season!

The End.

Check out the Bootsie website
www.bootsiebooks.com

Thanks to KooGa Rugby

www.kooga.com.au

CPSIA information can be obtained at www.ICGtesting.com
Printed in the USA
LVOW040422270212

270555LV00003B/3/P